Poems Book

By David Evans

Table of Contents

Wolf Poem

As I live among my pack, I feel a sense of great control and I can feel pack spirit.

Let the great pack spirit teach me how to hunt.

Let my pack remain young and let them live a life of pride and joy.

This is how my pack chooses to live.

Time to go on a great hunt.

Let's observe the alpha wolf and let her rule over me.

So, we choose to let her hunt and make a selection of prey she is going to hunt down.

Let us be patient with each other as we chow down on the great elk.

Elk you have given us life and sustainability for a day.

For we are a pack and will always remain a pack.

Angel Poem

I'm in your arms and I feel pleasantly relaxed flap those great wings of holiness.

I can see heaven above and I know someday that's where my journey will end.

I'm wrapped up in the holy white light, and I feel like anything is possible for me.

In the distance I can see more Angels rising up and taking lost souls along with them up to heaven.

Arch Angels please protect me from the demons below me.

Let me walk firmly on the ground and heal me while I walk along the road of desperation and hope.

Let me show non-believers that Angels exist and are here to help us heal and learn.

For I have learned to trust and love the Angels, I wish that I could never leave the arms of an Angel.

The Angels have taught me much about life and how to be a man of God.

Each Angel is different than the last, they all have their own special personality.

I love to be surrounded by white light and it keeps my mind on track.

Apple Tree Poem

I have strong roots and many long out reaching branches, I'm shorter than most oak trees.

Flowers bloom on the end of my branches, the bees visit me once a year and pollinate my flowers.

I'm a hardy tree that must be trimmed to keep me from growing too many sucker branches, that can overtake me.

I bare fruit in the summer months, my fruit is picked by hand.

I live in the Eastern USA and some places in between.

Fresh red delicious apples form from the blooming white flowers.

So come one come all to pick the sweet apples from my branches.

Don't let the apples fall upon your head and don't climb up me.

I'm just an apple tree that begs respect.

The caterpillars and I don't get along, the caterpillars infect my branches and chew up all my green branches causing them to fall apart.

I don't get along very well caterpillar, that's why I must be sprayed with pesticides to keep the intruders away from me.

Although I'm usually grown together with other trees, sometimes I'm just a lone tree. Everyone loves the fruit that I produce.

Blue Jay Poem

Fly through the sky oh great blue jay.

You have flown so high in the sky.

Lower your altitude, oh great blue jay and fly to me.

Let's fly away, into the blue sky, nothing but sky that I see.

There's a butterfly high in the sky and there's nothing but joy and happiness that I see.

I can hear the blue jays screeching and I see them flying in.

Let's watch them screech and play games with the other birds.

Now this is living, what a good life it's been.

The blue jays keep me company and make me such a happy fellow.

Oh, you great blue jays have made me smile so far.

Bravery Poem

I’m in a time of war and I’m determined to change the outcome of the war.

I have an iron will and would give my life to save another brother in arms along with me if I have to.

I would take a bullet for my fellow soldier and help strive through times of loss and hopelessness.

For I’m marine and always will be a marine.

It's my duty to stand up and fight even when others may not.

I’m a hero in my peer’s minds, I’ll reach a certain point and blossom into a fine fighter.

For I have overwhelming strength and fortitude.

I’m war hardened and I stand my ground fearlessly.

I stand tall with my rifle by my side and keep my head up.

I’m a positive soldier and will remain battle ready.

From my training I’m ready to fight with all that I have inside of me.

In my mind I’m a mighty warrior.

I’ll never give up or give in, I have courage and aren’t afraid to show.

When you think it's all over I’ll be there to save you.

I’ll fight on until I have no fight left in me.

I’m a US Marine; some call me a leather neck and a devil dog.

I’m not in it for the glory, I’m in it to save our fellow Americans.

I’m victorious and have gratitude towards the past generations who have fought to make America the one nation under God.

God bless those who didn’t make it back, for they were the true heroes.

Let their souls find the peace they are looking for; God bless the USA.

Dog Poem

The love from a dog is never ending, and they're always by your side looking up at you with a loving look.

For your dog is always there for you and doesn't leave you in a situation alone.

We need to learn from our pets, if they could talk they would have a lot to say I'm sure.

A dog is trustworthy and bring us great joy and hope into our lives.

Even though a dog lives not as long as we hope it would.

Dogs don't lie or cheat or leave us.

Dogs are so amazing; they're considered to be man's best friend.

A dog will do anything he can to bring a smile to someone's face.

Dogs have such a big heart and love us for who we truly are and they don't care about how we look.

They don't judge us like we judge each other and they don't care what color our skin is.

There is much to be said about dogs.

People say we are the most intelligent kind of beings out there, but if we don't start treating each other with respect we will soon perish.

Oh, great dog teach me your ways and your great patience and I give you all the love that I have in my heart.

Heaven and Earth Poem

There's a great Heaven above, the white light wraps itself around you while you're in Heaven.

The great beautiful Angels of Heaven are always looking down on you.

Oh, great Angels watch over me and my family and keeps us wrapped in healing white light.

I can feel the Angels surrounding me and I feel great peach and joy, you have saved me great Angels of Heaven.

Search for those that don't know God and bring them to me.

The healing white light is always surrounding me, while I'm living here on Earth.

Let the great healing energy cover our nation, our nation needs help.

Oh, great Angels step by our sides and lead us to a world filed with hope and violence can't no longer live in this world.

I can imagine the white loving light covering our nation, almost like a blanket.

Us beings will all eventually go to Heaven, after the Angels take us up to Heaven.

I see the lights coming down, from the Heavens.

Let the white light heal me and make me feel the way I should.

My faith is leading me to want to bask in the white light. God bless to all and all a good life.

Jesus Poem

I'm the son of God, I was a great healer, I was known as the king of the Jews.

I looked to the Heavens for guidance.

Mary had given birth to me.

I was born in a manager along with some farm animals.

I helped non-believers to see the light.

I would cure those who were sick and dying, I could heal someone just by looking at them or holding their hands.

I loved to help out strangers and would help protect them.

I don't believe in stoning anyone to death.

I have a pure heart and want to keep in good standing with the people.

I'm a direct threat to Rome.

The Romans can't understand who I am and all the great things I have done for the people.

They want to find me and find a way to prosecute me.

They succeeded in taking my Earthly body, but they didn't defeat me.

I rose from the dead-on Easter morning.

I made water into wine and had bread rain down from the Heavens to help to feed the masses.

I had no fears of death, I lived my life for the people.

My Earthly body was crucified and tortured until it gave up.

Although I'm still alive, I'm the one who helped people to become Christians.

I showed fishermen how to fish and I helped them to catch a boat full of fish.

Everyone who came in contact with me, learned a lesson and their lives were changed.

God knew what was going to happen to me in the end.

I died for the great sins of man.

Although I'm not done yet, I'll come back again when judgement day comes and I'll save the followers of Christ.

Strength Poem

You have to rise up from failure and move on, I stand here as if I were a fierce grizzly bear defending my ground with my life.

I'm all mighty and powerful, you can hear me roar.

I'm a fierce competitor and will never back down, and let my presence be known.

I have the strength to overcome any obstacle that may stand in my way.

I reach for the stars and I know I can reach them. I'm strong willed and won't allow myself to be pushed around.

As I rest I can feel my bodies determination growing in leaps and bounds.

Now I rise and take in the fresh air of success.

I'm a success and will keep on a positive uplifting trail.

I won't be overcome by any threatening presence.

I'm a warrior; I'm a being of higher reason.

I see no more sorrow or pain; I'm standing tall and tall I shall stand.

I can hear the voice of reason in my mind.

I'm not bewildered and won't let myself down, I'll fight through the hardest of hard situations.

I'll be brought to the light.

The Eagle Poem

Watch as the great majestic eagle soars so high in the blue sky.

Watch him soar to the Heavens and back.

You're a symbol of freedom in this great nation, I feel free as I watch you come in for a landing.

Oh, great eagle you rise from your ashes to live out the rest of your years.

Now you rise again just like Jesus did so many centuries ago.

Oh, great Eagle let me learn your teachings.

Come forth great wise spirit of the eagle.

Rose Poem

I'm a red flower, who is prettier than most. I grow among other roses in a rose garden.

I have thorns that grow on my green leaves.

I have a long green stem that's strong and helps me to support the weight of the large, beautiful flower.

I'm picked and given to the sweethearts of men.

Although after I'm picked I don't last very long in a vase.

I live for a week then my rose pedals begin to get droopy and I no longer look nice, I come in a variety of different colors.

I'm sold in flower shops all over town and the world.

In the wild I live out my days looking beautiful and swaying back and forth when the strong winds blow all around me.

I love when the sunlight beads down on my lovely bright green leaves.

I enjoy a nice summer shower that lasts just long enough to water me.

The fresh rainwater runs down my flower and stem and makes me feel full of energy.

I know that I'm one with nature.

I'm a plant that listens to my own reasons and do what I have to, to survive.

Summertime Poem

I feel the warm sunshine upon me, and what a nice breeze that I feel.

Life is good and so is the summer, for I most soak up the Sun's rays all summer long.

Let me take a dive in my pool and be refreshed and relaxed.

Oh, how I enjoy the eighty-degree weather, and I feel relaxed.

What a dreamy summer it's been, we're going to have some fun this summer.

Summer rolls on like thunder.

Thunder is short lived and is gone before you know it.

Let's go on a surfing safari and had ourselves a good and rich time in the summertime.

The summertime is rolling and rocking on.

Shall we rock and roll or just roll?

Let's roll down the road and put the windows down and put the radio on.

For its summertime and I'm loving it, gather one gather all for the summertime celebration.

It's time to celebrate the good times in the hot summer air.

Listen to nature and get a tan, it's the way of the summertime days.

Oh, sweet summertime I'm going to have the summertime blues in the wintertime.

Now I know that I'm leaving the summertime celebration looking for some new.

Now were calling upon wintertime once more or what a joy that is.

Tiger Poem

As I wander along the forest I think about my everlasting hunger and the method I'm going to use to attack my prey.

I love to stalk along and think about my next move.

I'm a tireless hunter who chooses his moves very carefully.

My senses have notified me of danger.

I must be hunted by a human hunter.

I better watch my steps and stay in the shadows.

I keep myself hidden for good reason, and I wish to stay safe while I'm on the hunt.

For I'm all about the hunt.

I'm on the hunt most of the time, and don't mind to stay on the trail on of my prey.

With my keen ability to stalk I can get close to my prey without them even knowing I'm there hiding in the shadows.

Nights are the best for me for my specialized eyes can see better than my preys.

What fun a night hunt for me is, for my prey has nowhere to turn and I can catch them.

My claws are sharp and I use them with great accuracy to take down my prey.

I have a great roar that is ferocious and can scare away my foes.

I live among my foes and have no fear of them.

I keep on thinking and stay hidden from my foes.

I need to remain as sly as a fox to outwit my foes.

Time Poem

The time passes by so fast where has it gone.

For time never ends and you stuck in a world of time.

Where have the years gone and what has happened to my body.

As time goes on I began to feel my age and the Earth years.

What has happened to just a minute?

Now you hear people say wait a second and once they have said that the second is up.

All we are is dust in the wind and eventually we lose to time. Time is like the grim reaper it comes upon you so quickly and it surprises you each and every day.

We all have a time to live and the time to die.

Time is a forward force that doesn't stop no matter what.

We must do things in a timely manner and that includes everything that we do in a days' time.

Time does not run backwards just forward.

Time makes me feel like I'm in a rush.

Time makes me learn to love the time I have left on earth.

Time is such an extreme factor in this life.

Our life is just an Allusion and there are plenty of parallel universes that are timeless.

Just think if there was no time, where would we be? Would we survive a timeless life?

What a crazy question that is.

Time is never wasted while I'm in a work mood.

Time has left me with no choose but to rush time and live on.

Let time go hence I know my life experience is only temporary.

Time goes by but we don't always seem to realize what had happened in that time.

As I pass into other realms of life I see a slowdown in earth time.

Rainbow Poem

I’m a natural occurring wonder, I come in all colors.

When people see me they’re filled with joy and become very happy with my presence.

I’m only around for a short period of time.

I can appear wherever and whenever when the conditions are right.

People have been seeing me for as long as humans have been living here on earth.

Some people think I’m magical and that when I appear a bucket of gold should appear right below me, but that’s not the way it works.

Songs have been written about me.

It doesn’t matter what the time of the year it is, I can appear in any season.

If you live up in Alaska you can see the Northern lights, they are very similar to me.

They can be all the colors of the rainbow just like me.

When I appear, I can be small or a larger size.

I'm in an arch formation and remain that way the whole time I'm there.

I bring smiles to children's faces and cheer people up.

Some people even think that when I appear I mean good luck.

I'm seen before or after a good rain or even after a snowstorm.

The temperature doesn't bother me.

I sometimes appear after the fog has settled and gone away.

I'm seen all over the world.

Photographers enjoy to take my picture whenever they are observing me.

Pumpkin Poem

I'm orange and are plump, I grow in a patch called a pumpkin patch.

I'm in the gourd family and can grow to large proportions.

I'm harvested around the fall time of year.

People place me as a decoration besides their front door.

People carve me up and then call me a jackalope and lit up a candle and place it inside of me.

After I'm carved I don't last but a few days.

People enjoy to eat my seeds, horror stories have been written about me.

I'm not evil like they show in the horror films the farmer harvests me in a peaceful manner.

He comes down to the pumpkin patch early in the morning.

I make children happy when they see me.

I'm launched out of cannons at the various pumpkin contests.

I can grow to a small petite size or I can grow larger than a truck.

Grasshopper Poem

I'm green and have six legs, I have two long antennas that extend out from my head.

I have a longer body then most insects, I have two big eyes so that I can see you better.

I have two long powerful back legs that help me to hop and to catapult myself up into the air.

You can find me in field of long grass.

I like to perch myself on the edge of a large leaf.

I have many predators and I keep an eye on them.

I can fly short distances and my wings fold up when I'm done flying, my long front legs help me to keep my balance.

I avoid coming in contact with spiders or any other kind of carnivorous insect.

I'm on their menu so I must keep myself out of harm's way.

I like to eat plants so I'm called a plant eater.

My legs allow me to jump up to a meter high.

I am proud of my jumping ability.

When I jump I have to go through a three-stage process, which isn't easy and takes some concentration to get the whole process underway.

Now for an applause as I get ready to jump, I did it and everyone applauded.

Kite Poem

I can be seen flying high in the sky in the park or any other recreational place.

I have been around since the early eighteen hundreds.

You have to hold onto me tightly or I'll fly away.

Don't let me go too high or I'll be in the clouds and away I'll go out of sight then out of mind.

I may come in different colors and different shapes.

I'm light and streamline and are easily taken by the slightest of winds.

I fly high above you and sometimes I get blown out beyond your reach.

Keep my string held tight in your hand and let me fly higher.

As I continue to fly high I go higher and higher until I go past the clouds.

I'm now above the clouds and are lost now.

As you began to relax you let go of the string and I flew far, far away and now I'm lost high in the sky.

Cheetah Poem

I'm a great cat and I travel at fast speeds while I go looking for prey.

I run on and on and have a good sense of direction.

As I run towards my prey I feel like I'm on the top of the world.

My sharp teeth and claws and speed make me a perfect predator for the Savannah.

The long savanna grass brushes up against my lean body as I run through it.

Now I have caught my prey and have beat the odds, I take time to chow down and get my body ready for the next great chase.

I have a streamlined body that's powerful and I have a fierce attitude that carries me through the day to the next chase.

As I run along the great Savannah I feel a sense of uncontrolled power and can feel the connect between me and Mother Earth.

Let my foes watch on as I beat all the odds that are against.

Come on great lions of the plains, let's see your dominance over this land.

Listen to your great roar, you're the king of the jungle and the plains.

For I stand down to you oh great lions, let's feast together and still remain fierce competitors.

Space Poem

While I'm suspended high in space.

I feel alone and lost in the cold dark reaches of space.

It's just empty space and nothing is around you.

As you float along in the dark reaches of space you feel overwhelmed by darkness that never becomes light.

Where's the mighty light from the sun? It's seems to be lost and hope of light is long gone.

You're now floating past the many planets that make up our solar system.

You can learn a lot from observing the planets, it's cold in dark space and there is not light.

You need a ray of hope that will come from the mighty sun.

Where's thy mighty sun?

Oh, there it is peeking around the great red planet Mars.

Let's check out the everlasting light from the sun.

Oh, great star of hope, I'm warmed by your rays of hope.

Duckling Poem

I follow the path of my mom and other siblings.

I have soft yellow feathers; I'm young and haven't reached adult hood.

I follow my mom to where we swim and socialize with the other ducks in the local pond.

I haven’t earned my wings yet but am looking forward to flight, flight is so important to me.

I waddle around with my siblings and don't know who else to follow.

I’m a follower not a leader, at least not yet.

I’m not adventurous and prefer to waddle around and stay safe with my mom and siblings.

I haven’t swam across the pond yet, today I learned how to swim along with my family.

Mom always warns of us of danger, oh what a life it is.

I’m tiny and know my place in the food chain.

People have tried to make rubber duckies look like me but they will never be as cute or as fluffy as I am.

I love to cuddle and waddle around.

I consider myself to be a cute duckling not an ugly duckling.

I know I’m cute and let it get to my head.

I’m observed each day, by the people who visit the pond everyday that's in the park.

I walk around the pond every day and get noticed by the happy city folk.

I bring smiles and giggles to little boys and girls every time they see me.

They point out and mention me to their parents. Everyone loves a duckling, whether it's ugly or not.

I'm a duckling and like to swim around in the water, I sometimes splash around when my mom is not looking.

I like to get caught in the middle of the rainstorm, and waddle around and feel the cold rain come down and run down my feathers.

I'm a duckling who doesn't take chances, I have been known to cross the roadways with my mother and siblings.

I like to eat bread when it's thrown at me from a gracious human.

I'm a demanding duckling.

I like to play a game where I duck in and out between the giant human's legs.

I'll soon lose my cute yellow feathers and grow ugly ones.

Crow Poem

My feathers are all black, people have an eerie feeling about me.

My eyes are all black and this spooks a lot of people when they look into my eyes and see nothing but black.

I have a long black beak that's sharp.

My talons are so very sharp and help me to grasp onto my prey or other things.

I'm squawk and my call can be heard for miles.

This makes some people get shivers down their spine.

I have played a star role in horror movies and my counterpart the raven was made famous in horror movies also.

I can be a pest to other birds, and I like to perch myself on whatever I can.

Sometimes I'll have fights with other birds while in midair.

I peck at them and let out an annoying screech at them.

Although I'm feared and not really understood by people I'm a natural garbage man.

I'm considered to be a scavenger and I eat the dead things that are left unclaimed.

I have good eyesight but not as good as an Eagles.

I like to eat what I can find and are not a picky eater.

I don't mind picking the bones of a dead animal.

I don't taste the food, but just eat it anyway.

If I choose I can fly high in the sky and go on my own adventures.

I'm not the biggest sized bird, the largest bird that lives today is the California Condor.

Some people mistaken me for a Raven, but that's alright and understandable.

www.ingramcontent.com/pod-product-compliance
Lightning Source LLC
LaVergne TN
LVHW040936150826
845672LV00007B/2393

* 9 7 9 8 8 4 5 9 8 9 1 5 4 *